BLOOMSBURY PAPERBACKS

THIS BLOOMSBURY BOOK
BELONGS TO

....

KOZZEE
BOOSTER
PADS
BABY
SUPER
NAPPIES

d
d
SUPER
NAPPIES
BABY
KOZZEE
BOOSTER
PADS

TO EMMA AND ELSIE – M.R.

FOR TOBY AND THE TANGERINE TOWEL – N.L.

BLOOMSBURY CHILDREN'S BOOKS

First published in Great Britain in 2004 by Bloomsbury Publishing Plc
38 Soho Square, London, W1D 3HB
This paperback edition first published in 2005

A CIP catalogue record of this book is available from the British Library

ISBN 0 7475 7137 6

Printed and bound in China by South China Printing Co

1 3 5 7 9 10 8 6 4 2

All papers used by Bloomsbury Publishing are natural, recyclable products made from wood
grown in well-managed forests. The manufacturing processes conform to the
environmental regulations of the country of origin.

Howler

Michael Rosen Neal Layton

Hello. I write books. I like things to mean just what they are supposed to mean.

Rover is a small human and she is my pet.
Rover is the name that I gave her.
But it doesn't stop there. Oh no.

Rover has a dad
who barks a lot.
I call him Rex.

I call Rover's
mum Cindy.

Rex and Cindy and Rover aren't the only people in this book.
I am in it too. Oh yes.

I have a good story to tell today.

It all began when I noticed one day that Cindy was getting bigger.

She didn't get bigger upwards.

She started getting bigger outwards.

BIGGER

I thought she had swallowed a big dinner.
But she kept on getting bigger.
Bigger and bigger and bigger.

The next thing I noticed was that Rex came back with a new basket for me.

But every time I tried to get in it, they all barked at me.
Loudly.

Then they hung small animals from the ceiling.
I found out they were too high up to chase.

I think I started to understand what was going on when
Cindy gave Rover a book full of very small humans.

Then one day I took Rover to stay with the big human next door. I call her Trixie. Rex and Cindy went off quickly in the family box. Cindy was breathing loudly.

Rover and Trixie pretended to be Rex and Cindy and squeezed my rabbit.

Rover looked worried.

When Rex and Cindy came back they had found a very small human. Rover stared at it. Rover tried to eat it. It tried to eat Cindy.

Most of the time it howled. So I called it Howler. Rex slept.
And no one noticed me.

No one at all.

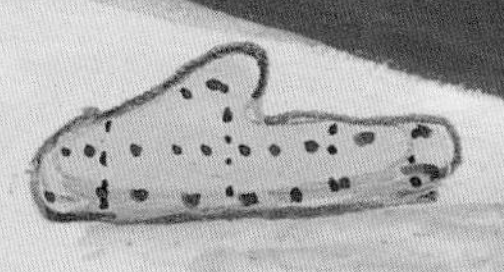

I tried wagging my tail.
I went and got the ball in case they had lost it.
I hunted my tail very quickly.

But no matter what I did, no one noticed me.

It was time to do something about it. My first plan was to tell Howler to go. Rex woke up and sent me out.

My next plan was to tell Rex and Cindy to go.
Rex woke up again and sent me out.

And then I came up with my great plan. I got friendly with Ruff-ruff. Her pet human is Trixie. So while Rex and Cindy and Rover were busy with Howler, I spent some time with my friend, Ruff-ruff.

Not long after Ruff-ruff got bigger. Not longwards. Outwards. And then one day she had five small ones. Ruff-ruff called them Rufflets. I thought they all ought to be called Small Me, but I wasn't asked.

Rover came and looked at the Rufflets and barked.
Rex woke up. He came and looked and barked.
Cindy came to look. She barked. Trixie came to look.
She barked.

Everyone came to look. Except for Howler.

Then I made up my mind. I think that as long as Rex and Cindy and Rover and Trixie say it's OK for the Rufflets to stay, then it's OK for Howler to stay.

I won't tell Howler to go. But maybe that's because I know who Rover likes best.

KOZZEE
BOOSTER
PADS
BABY
U U
SUPER
NAPPIES

SUPER NAPPIES
BABY
KOZZEE
BOOSTER
PADS

Enjoy more great picture books from Michael Rosen and Neal Layton ...

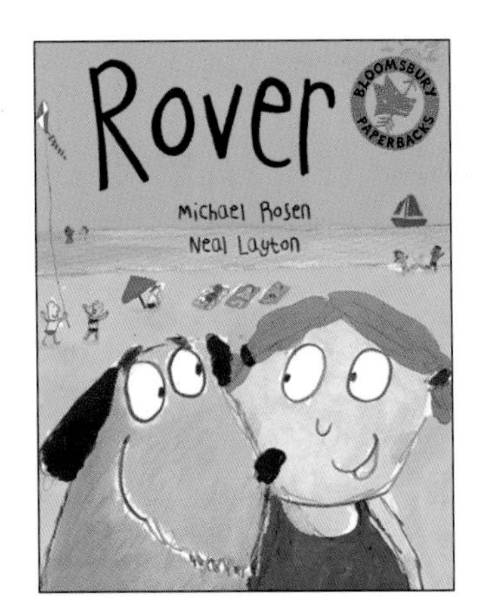

ROVER
Michael Rosen & Neal Layton

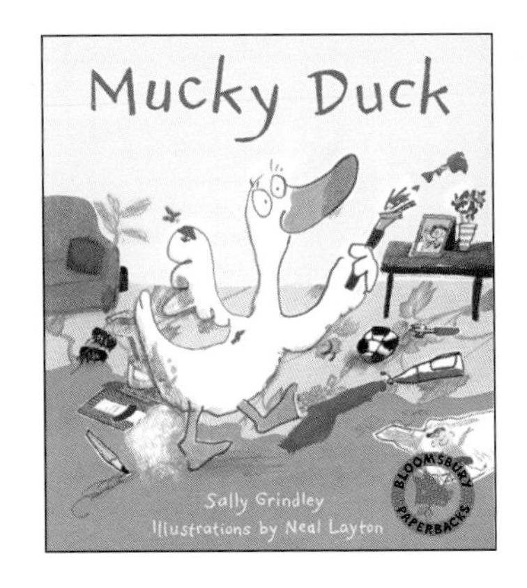

MUCKY DUCK
Sally Grindley & Neal Layton

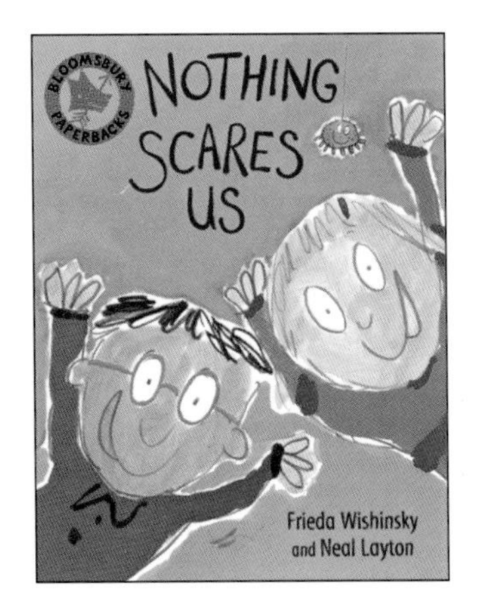

NOTHING SCARES US
Frieda Wishinsky & Neal Layton

THE PHOTO
Neal Layton

All now available in paperback